Dedicated to the Cats Protection League
for our lovely cat, Bluebell —C. H.

To find out more about the Cats Protection League visit:
www.cats.org.uk

For Rita —E. U.

Text copyright © 2017 by Caryl Hart
Illustrations copyright © 2017 by Lisa Jones Studio

First published in Great Britain in August 2017 by Bloomsbury Publishing Plc
Published in the United States of America in July 2018
by Bloomsbury Children's Books
www.bloomsbury.com

Bloomsbury is a registered trademark of Bloomsbury Publishing Plc

For information about permission to reproduce selections from this book, write to
Permissions, Bloomsbury Children's Books, 1385 Broadway, New York, New York 10018
Bloomsbury books may be purchased for business or promotional use. For information on bulk purchases please contact
Macmillan Corporate and Premium Sales Department at specialmarkets@macmillan.com

Library of Congress Cataloging-in-Publication Data
Names: Hart, Caryl, author. | Underwood, Edward (Illustrator), illustrator.
Title: Big box little box / by Caryl Hart ; illustrated by Edward Underwood.
Description: New York : Bloomsbury, 2018.
Summary: A curious cat investigates every box it can find—and makes a mouse friend along the way.
Identifiers: LCCN 2017047798 (print) | LCCN 2017061813 (e-book)
ISBN 978-1-68119-786-9 (hardcover)
ISBN 978-1-68119-913-9 (e-book) • ISBN 978-1-68119-914-6 (e-PDF)
Subjects: | CYAC: Cats—Fiction. | Boxes—Fiction.
Classification: LCC PZ7.H25633 Bi 2018 (print) | LCC PZ7.H25633 (e-book) | DDC [E]—dc23
LC record available at https://lccn.loc.gov/2017047798

Art created with pencil, ink, and computer-assisted collage
Typeset in Filosofia
Book design by Goldy Broad
Printed in China by Leo Paper Products, Heshan, Guangdong
2 4 6 8 10 9 7 5 3 1

BIG BOX LITTLE BOX

illustrated by

Caryl Hart   Edward Underwood

BLOOMSBURY
NEW YORK LONDON OXFORD NEW DELHI SYDNEY

Big box

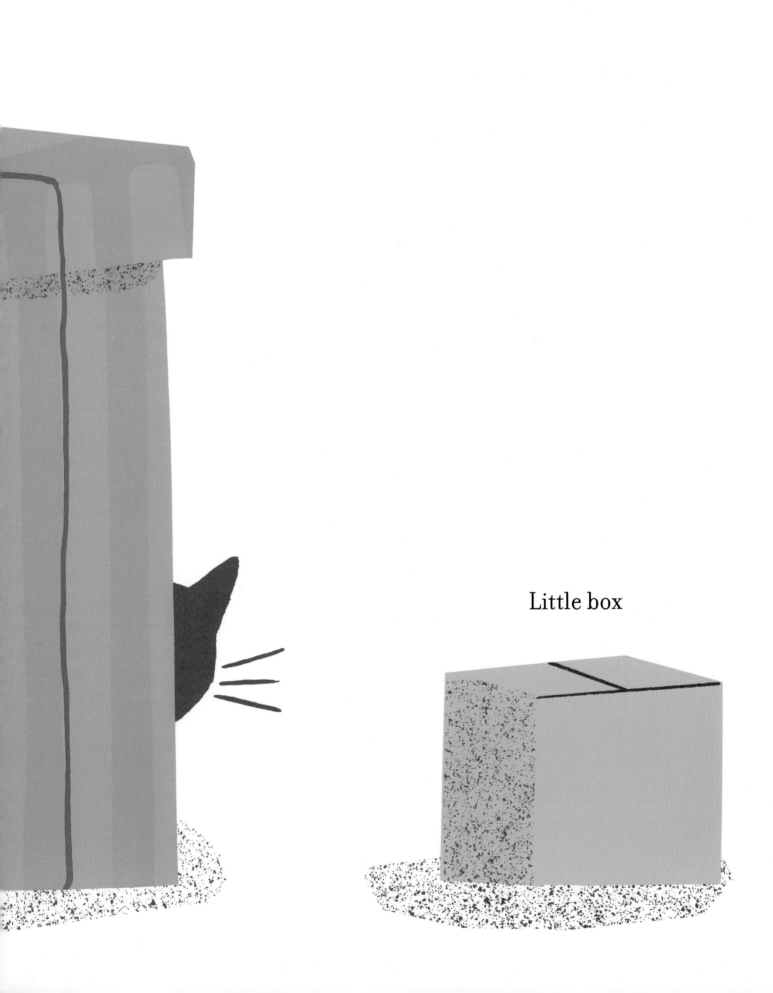

Little box

HUGE box

Tiny box

Thin box

Fat box

Cat box?

Flat box

Brown box

Green box

Yellow box

Black box

Blue box

Red box

Hey! That's not a BED box!

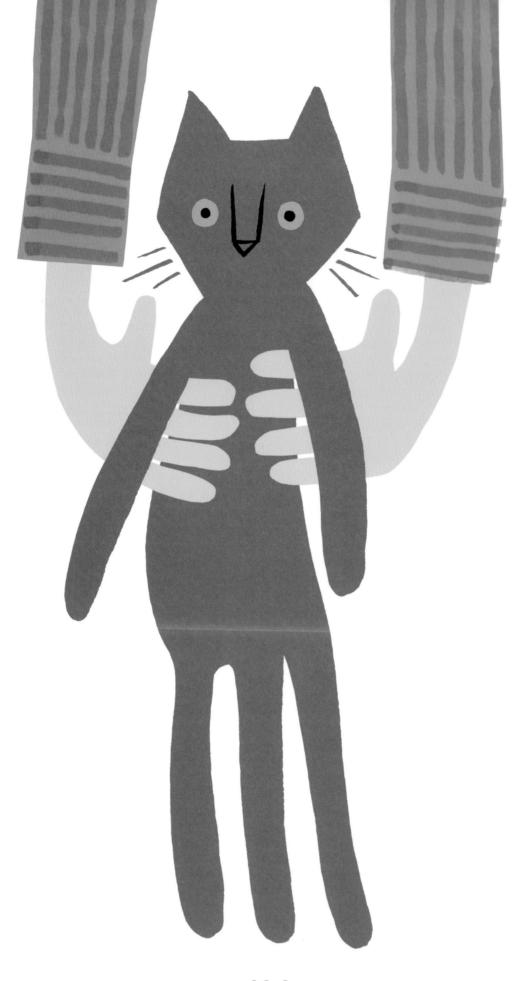

My box

YOUR box

ZZZZZZZZ

Snore box

Plain box

Jazzy box

Spotty box

Snazzy box

Shoe box?

Hat box?

Perfect for a
cat box

Slippy box

Slidey box

Run away and hidey box

Box round

Box square

This one has a hole
right there!

Nibbled box

Chewed box

Food box?

House box?

MOUSE BOX!

Cat peeks

Mouse squeaks

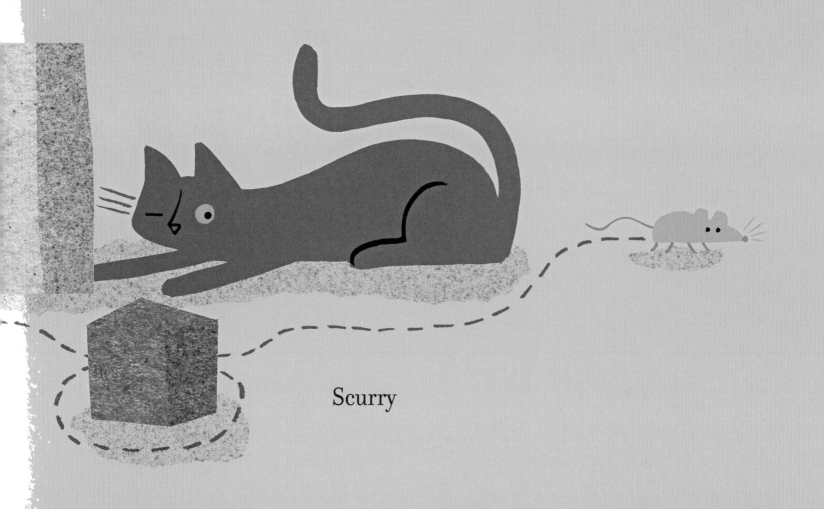

Scurry

Pounce

Chase

Bounce

Tickle

Purr

Warm fur

New friends

ENDS